TODAY'S HITS
Playalong *for* Alto Saxophone

WISE PUBLICATIONS
London/New York/Paris/Sydney/Copenhagen/Madrid/Tokyo

Exclusive Distributors:
Music Sales Limited
8/9 Frith Street, London W1D 3JB, England.
Music Sales Pty Limited
120 Rothschild Avenue, Rosebery, NSW 2018, Australia.

Order No. AM966031
ISBN 0-7119-8363-1
This book © Copyright 2001 by Wise Publications.

Compiled by Nick Crispin.
Music arranged by Simon Lesley.
Music processed by Enigma Music Production Services.
Cover photography by George Taylor.
Printed in the United Kingdom by Page Bros., Norwich, Norfolk.

CD produced by Jonas Persson.
Instrumental solos by John Whelan.
All guitars by Arthur Dick.
Engineered by Kester Sims.

Your Guarantee of Quality:
As publishers, we strive to produce every book to
the highest commercial standards.
The music has been freshly engraved and the book has been
carefully designed to minimise awkward page turns and
to make playing from it a real pleasure.
Particular care has been given to specifying acid-free, neutral-sized
paper made from pulps which have not been elemental chlorine bleached.
This pulp is from farmed sustainable forests and was
produced with special regard for the environment.
Throughout, the printing and binding have been planned to
ensure a sturdy, attractive publication which should give years of enjoyment.
If your copy fails to meet our high standards,
please inform us and we will gladly replace it.

Music Sales' complete catalogue describes thousands of
titles and is available in full colour sections by subject,
direct from Music Sales Limited.
Please state your areas of interest and send a
cheque/postal order for £1.50 for postage to:
Music Sales Limited, Newmarket Road, Bury St. Edmunds, Suffolk IP33 3YB.

www.musicsales.com

Saxophone Fingering Chart

LIGATURE

MOUTHPIECE

CROOK

THUMB SUPPORT

BODY

1L

2L
3L
1ST FINGER

4L

5L
2ND FINGER
3RD FINGER
6L
7L
8L
9L

LEFT HAND

OCTAVE KEY

THUMB REST

1R

2R

3R

*4R

1ST FINGER

5R
2ND FINGER

3RD FINGER
6R
7R

RIGHT HAND

THE RING

* Not fitted on some saxophones

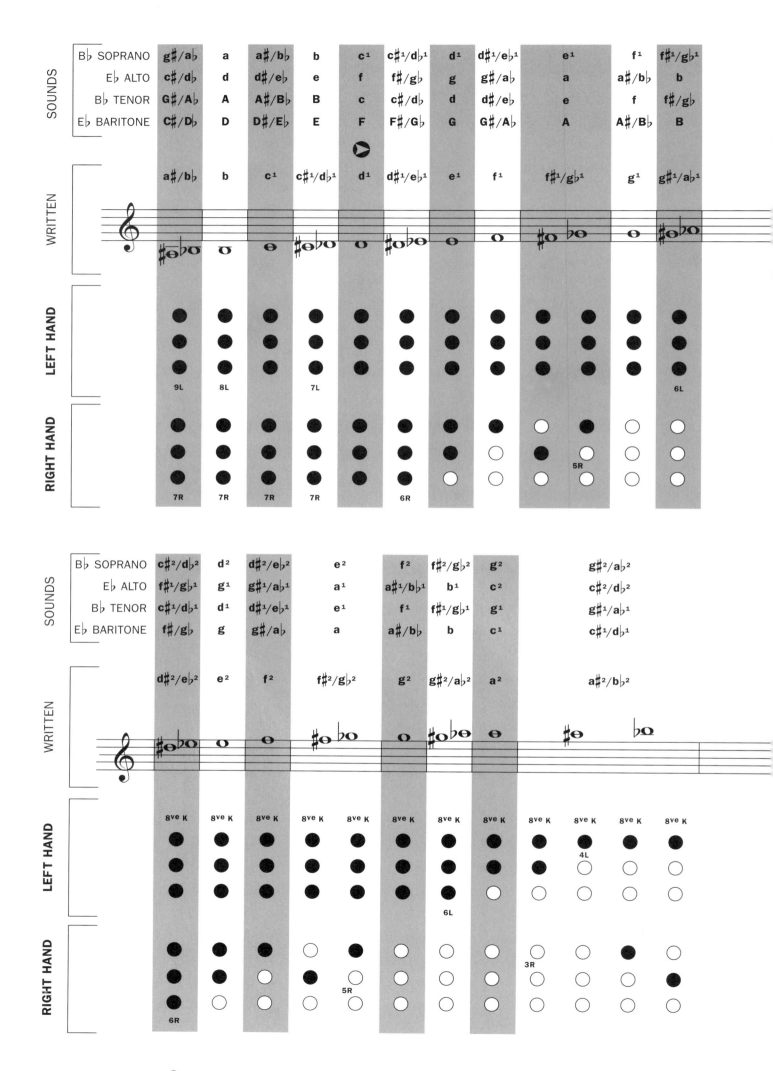

Indicates the lower limit of the best playing range

g¹ g#¹/ab¹ a¹ a#¹/bb¹ b¹ c²

c¹ c#¹/db¹ d¹ d#¹/eb¹ e¹ f¹

g g#/ab a a#/bb b c¹

c c#/db d d#/eb e f

a¹ a#¹/bb¹ b¹ c² c#²/db² d²

8ve K   8ve K

4L

7L

3R   2R

7R

a² a#²/bb² b² c³ c#³/db³ d³ d#³/eb³

d² d#²/eb² e² f² f#²/gb² g² g#²/ab²

a¹ a#¹/bb¹ b¹ c² c#²/db² d² d#²/eb²

d¹ d#¹/eb¹ e¹ f¹ f#¹/gb¹ g¹ g#¹/ab¹

b² c³ c#³/db³ d³ d#³/eb³ e³ f³

8ve K 8ve K 8ve K 8ve K 8ve K 8ve K 8ve K 8ve K 8ve K 8ve K

1L   1L

3L   2L   2L   2L
     3L   3L   3L
               5L

2R   1R   1R

Indicates the upper limit of the best playing range

Eternal Flame

Words & Music by Billy Steinberg, Tom Kelly & Susanna Hoffs

Let Love Be Your Energy

Words & Music by Robbie Williams & Guy Chambers

9

Don't Stop Movin'

Words & Music by Simon Ellis, Sheppard Solomon & S Club 7

quasi improvised solo

non legato

sub. **ff**

f

3

mp

Out Of Reach

Words & Music by Gabrielle & Jonathan Shorten

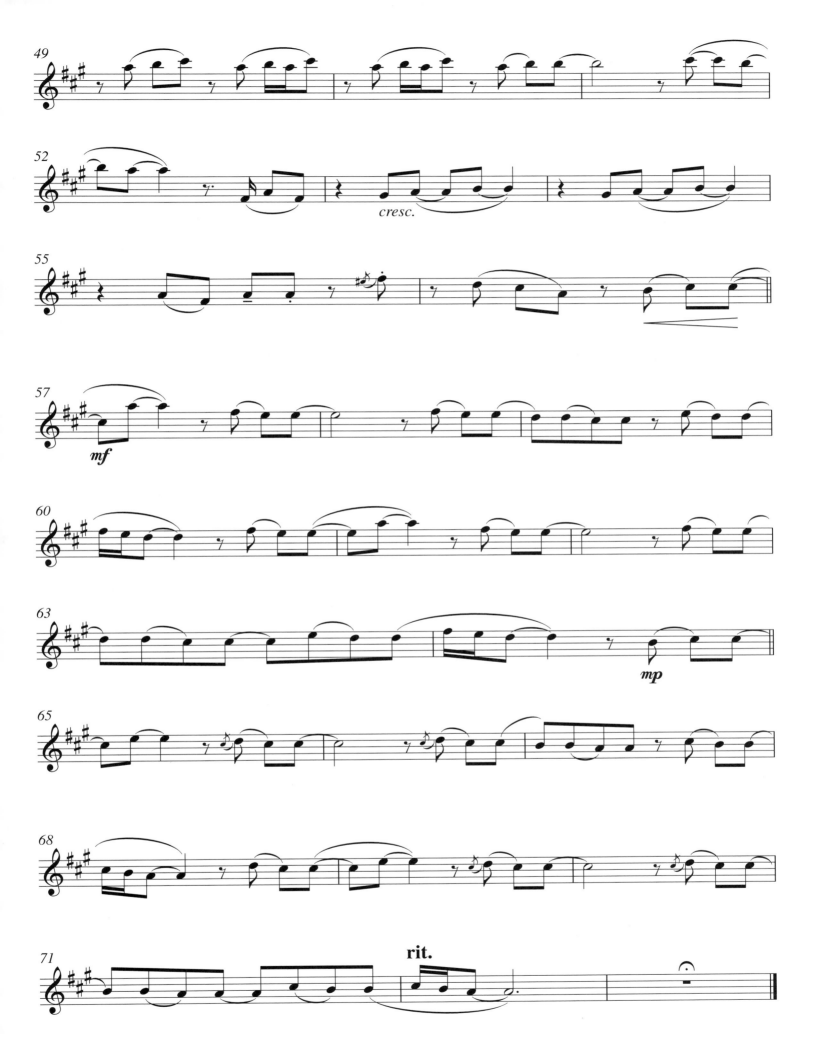

Only For A While

Words & Music by Joseph Washbourn

Step into the spotlight with...

GUEST SPOT

...and playalong *with* the specially recorded backing tracks

A great book and CD series,
each title available in arrangements for
FLUTE, CLARINET, ALTO SAXOPHONE,
TENOR SAXOPHONE*, TRUMPET* and **VIOLIN***

Pull Out

Now you can own professiona

when you play all thes

for Clarinet, Flute, Alto Saxophon

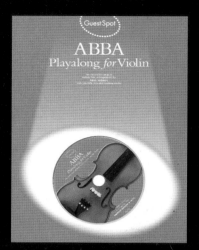

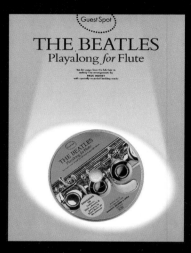

The *essential* book & CD series...

From Jazz, Blues and Swing to Ballads, Showstoppers, Film and TV Themes, here are all your favourite Chart Hits and more! *Check out* the special editions featuring legends of pop, **Abba** and **The Beatles**.

The Music Book...

Top line arrangements for 10 songs, *plus* a fingering guide for wind instruments.

The CD...

Hear full performance versions of all the songs. Then play along with the recorded accompaniments.

ABBA

Includes:
Dancing Queen
Fernando
Mamma Mia
Waterloo

AM960905 Clarinet
AM960894 Flute
AM960916 Alto Saxophone
AM960927 Violin

BALLADS

Includes:
Candle In The Wind
Imagine
Killing Me Softly With His Song
Wonderful Tonight

AM941787 Clarinet
AM941798 Flute
AM941809 Alto Saxophone

THE BEATLES

Includes:
All You Need Is Love
Hey Jude
Lady Madonna
Yesterday

NO90682 Clarinet
NO90683 Flute
NO90684 Alto Saxophone

CHRISTMAS

Includes:
Frosty The Snowman
Have Yourself A Merry Little Christmas
Mary's Boy Child
Winter Wonderland

AM950400 Clarinet
AM950411 Flute
AM950422 Alto Saxophone

have your very

packing band...

reat melody line arrangements

enor Saxophone*, Trumpet* and Violin*

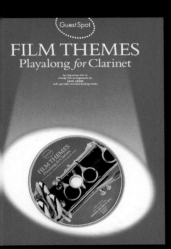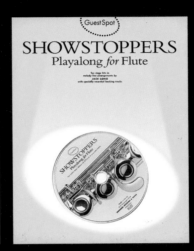

CLASSIC BLUES

Includes:
ever
arlem Nocturne
Moonglow
ound Midnight

M941743 Clarinet
M941754 Flute
M941765 Alto Saxophone

CLASSICS

ncludes:
ir On The 'G' String - Bach
upiter (from The Planets Suite) -
Holst
Ode To Joy (Theme from
Symphony No.9 'Choral') -
Beethoven
Swan Lake (Theme) -
Tchaikovsky.

M955537 Clarinet
M955548 Flute
M955560 Violin

FILM THEMES

Includes:
Circle Of Life (The Lion King)
Love Is All Around
(Four Weddings & A Funeral)
Moon River
(Breakfast At Tiffany's)
You Must Love Me (Evita)

AM941864 Clarinet
AM941875 Flute
AM941886 Alto Saxophone

JAZZ

Includes:
Fly Me To The Moon
Opus One
Satin Doll
Straight No Chaser

AM941700 Clarinet
AM941710 Flute
AM941721 Alto Saxophone

NINETIES HITS

Includes:
Falling Into You (Celine Dion)
Never Ever (All Saints)
Tears In Heaven (Eric Clapton)
2 Become 1 (Spice Girls)

AM952853 Clarinet
AM952864 Flute
AM952875 Alto Saxophone

No.1 HITS

Includes:
A Whiter Shade Of Pale
(Procol Harum)
Every Breath You Take
(The Police)
No Matter What (Boyzone)
Unchained Melody
(The Righteous Brothers).

AM955603 Clarinet
AM955614 Flute
AM955625 Alto Saxophone
AM959530 Violin

SHOWSTOPPERS

Includes:
Big Spender (Sweet Charity)
Bring Him Home (Les Misérables)
I Know Him So Well (Chess)
Somewhere (West Side Story)

AM941820 Clarinet
AM941831 Flute
AM941842 Alto Saxophone

SWING

Includes:
I'm Getting Sentimental
Over You
Is You Is Or Is You Ain't
My Baby?
Perdido
Tuxedo Junction

AM949377 Clarinet
AM960575 Trumpet
AM949399 Alto Saxophone
AM959618 Tenor Saxophone

TV THEMES

Includes:
Black Adder
Home And Away
London's Burning
Star Trek

AM941908 Clarinet
AM941919 Flute
AM941920 Alto Saxophone

* Selected titles only

Sample the *whole* series of *Guest Spot* with these special double CD bumper compilations...

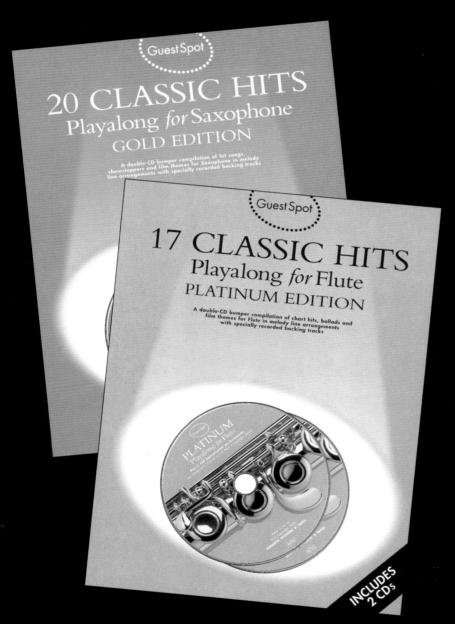

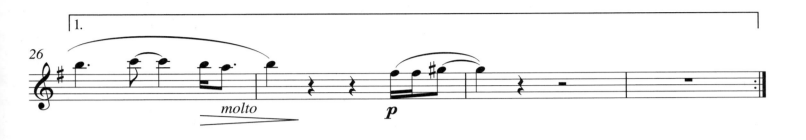

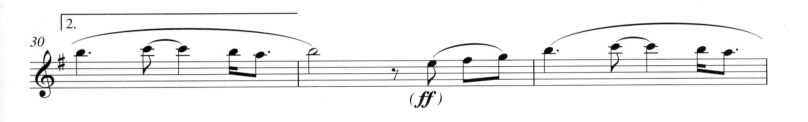

Run For Cover

Words & Music by Cameron McVey, Johnny Lipsey, Paul Simm, Siobhan Donaghy, Keisha Buchanan & Mutya Buena

Dance pop, sadly ♩ = 90

Sail Away

Words & Music by David Gray

Sing

Words & Music by Fran Healy

Pure And Simple

Words & Music by Tim Hawes, Pete Kirtley & Alison Clarkson

What Took You So Long?

Words & Music by Emma Bunton, Richard Stannard, Julian Gallagher, Martin Harrington, John Themis & Dave Morgan